# THINKY LINES ON INKY PAGES

Dr. Aparajita Chakraborty

First published in 2020 by
BecomeShakespeare.com

One Point Six Technologies Pvt Ltd,
123, Building J2, Shram Seva Premises,
Wadala Truck Terminus,
Wadala (E), Mumbai - 400037
T:+91 8080226699



ISBN: 978-93-90543-88-5

# — DEDICATIONS —

to My mother
Late Mrs. Arundhati Chakraborty

This poetry book is dedicated to few of the important persons who have played an inevitable role in molding my personality. They have persistently encouraged me to put in my continuous efforts. They taught me that an opportunity becomes the proof of our capability if we can try our level best .

Firstly, I would like to thank the Almighty.

Then I would like to thank my mother – late Mrs. Arundhati Chakraborty for her constant support and all tireless efforts. I will remember her words "be good, do good";

A big thanks goes to my father, Dr.Alok Ranjan Chakrraborty, who was the first listener of all the poems in the preparatory phase. He has been a continuous source of knowledge who believes that learning cannot be over in one lifetime.

I would thank my husband Mr.Bikramjit Acharyya for his constant support and motivation . He had the tolerance to listen to my poems over the phone and give any necessary idea to improve.

I thank my jethu, Dr. Giridhari Kar , a renowned physician and a versatile man who has been a constant source of optimism and appreciation right from my kinder garden days till today.

I would also like to thank former MP Mr. Kamalendu Bhattacharjee, who kindled an interest in English literature that persisted all along my medical school. I will remember his line "always answer in the language of the question".

And I would like to thank  Mr.Surajit Chakraborty and Mr.Gaurav Choudhury for the relentless support and help.

And I thank all my family and friends for their support in every possible way.

# THINKY LINES ON INKY PAGES

Thoughts come and thoughts go.  It is an awesome experience to grab some of  them and recreate some new ideas. One of such approach was to write down some simple poems including expression of certain emotions, with a note of positivity, and some unreal comparisons as a metaphor.

A few poems are also from the doctors chamber which try to relate medical conditions with non medical occurrences, both of which run parallel and simultaneously.

With every page, one new idea will emerge .  I welcome all of you to join in this new journey…

Dr. Aparajita Chakraborty, M.B.B.S, M.D (S.M.C ) ,F.I.Diab (UK) is a resident of Silchar , Assam, India. Presently she is working as a Demonstrator  in Silchar Medical College and Hospital. Before entering into the medical school, she graduated in painting, Kathak dance and Indian classical music and Rabindra sangeet and dance.

Though writing poems or articles was just confined before only to college magazines. Now in this festive season , here she makes an attempt to pen down her thoughts .

# TABLE OF CONTENTS

# 1

## KNOWLEDGE IS POWER, IGNORANCE IS BLISS

Mr or miss, ignorance is bliss,

I did not know when I would be born,

It  might be a dusk or might be a new dawn.

I was ignorant and yes, I was born.

I was born, I was happy and I felt that I was blessed;

I grew up , I knew nothing , till my eyes on her face fixed,

It  was my mother and I knew it was her,

Then I knew who I was and who were the others.

I knew what is good and then what is bad,

And along with happiness, I started knowing what is being sad.

I started learning, I started knowing,

Without which I couldnt keep growing,

With knowledge came anxiety, came a desire to know tomorrow,

And that spoilt my today ,I didn't know where I should go!

As I was ignorant about tomorrow, I never worried where I would go,

I enjoyed today, cherished yesterday and also smiled preparing for tomorrow.

Blessed are we all who don't know what in coming moments lie,

So life gives us chance to live,love, enjoy and die.

Live in your present, live in the skies;

Work for the moment as time always flies.

I may be with someone ,or may be with a phone,

One  fine morning my life will be gone.

All the while my thought should be one-

I wonder how knowledge can strengthen,

I wonder how ignorance can encourage!

I wish I were ignorant, I wish I were blessed,

With the growing knowledge, I always feel stressed.

Knowledge is power, let it shower,

Ignorance is bliss , let no one miss.

# 2

# TO DO OR NOT TO DO

The heart says to do one, the mind thinks along,

Life says to think again, mind finds a different song.

Goodness is what the heart wants, safety wants the mind,

Asleep are those in mother's lap, soldiers are of a different kind.

Truth makes the heart smile and mind seeks diplomacy,

Others say "forget the matter" and I feel the agony.

Love lights the candle and I feel the warmth,

Some may break my trust and I will feel the dearth.

Faith loves hope and they both make me strong,

The people in the chair prove my thoughts are wrong.

Men love money, as money is our need,

We misuse money and the mankind suffers indeed!

To love or not to love is what makes me mad,

Goodness is not appreciated which also makes me sad.

To be true or not to be, I always wonder,

I listen to my heart and let others wander.

To be good or not to be is a matter of choice,

If  you want to arise, you have to clear your voice.

Let love and hope hold the light, and faith show the way.

To do or not to do will be answered in its finest way.!

# 3

# THE TREE OF LIFE

Branches grew, so grew new leaves
Came out my new life, along with Ma's cries

Seasons change so changes tree's colour,
Also like that changes life's flavor

Bud it was which grew into a tree
Bound are we all till we become free

Green is the leaf ,so shall it turn yellow,
Alone we were born, so did our fellow.

Fruits come out of time and seasons
So comes solution with thoughts and passion

Red with flowers are the trees today,
Only branches and roots will be left one day

So is our life with youth and beauty,
All will finally go leaving tales of our done duty

Tasty be your fruits , dark be your shade
Love all people, let it not fade

Air that you purify, fodder that you provide,
Let our lives be useful for others and let no reason bring a divide!

Unity is strength , unity is power,
You believe in one blessing, others will soon shower

Trees will burn or be cut, a day will come when it will be gone,
So shall I and you will go, just like we came, we all will go

Be it fruits or be it flowers,colours and taste will be remembered,
Also like that our deeds will count ,duties praised and prayers revered.

# 4

## WHEN SEVEN SISTERS SING TOGETHER

The beauty of the hills,the smell of her tree,

The tune of her Bihu,guess where it can be?

**Assam** is our motherland, so it is here,

Success, silk, happiness and love is all that we care.

Such is her richness in music and rituals,

Held high is her history in heritage and spirituals

Rhinicerous grow and mighty river Brahmaputra with his tributaries do flow,

Many dance forms of her from many hearts do glow.

Rains and clouds, who desires to see

Hills and chills, guess the place it can be?

**Meghalaya** is a wonder where tourist can relax in a deep slumber.

Academics high,discipline sure, you need to ask what more for ?

Beautiful bamboo and beautiful artists work,

Kings and queens still reside on the earth.

**Tripura** is a miracle with soldiers on duty,

Even without residing there you can be proud of her beauty

Dance and shawls with hills standing perfect

**Nagaland** is the name I would like to direct.

Tunes run in her clouds, elegant beyond thoughts.

Sing in her praise ,without any doubt

Dancing with bamboo, claps everywhere,

Mizoram is the place you can think of nowhere

Orchids bloom and create a signature,

Nature is beautiful with every creature!

Vast are the Lokhtak lakes where horizon seems to fade,
Manipur is the place with martial arts of blade
Dresses and styles make all look pretty
Manipuri dance is classical with all beauty

Temples and monastery generate her scenery
Serene is their presence with surrounding greenery
Foothills of Himalayas and series of hills
God is the creator, blessed be his will
**Arunachal Pradesh** is the name with borders we care
Soldiers in her lap will stand in courage very fair.

Seven are we sisters, seven is our strength,
We form North Eastern India, many borders do we defend.
Soulful is our music, gorgeous is our culture
India is our country, very prayerful is is dear!

# 5

## MOTHER'S LOVE

My mother she became when I was born,

Blessed were our lives with desires to adorn,

She loved me more, she loved me a lot,

She loved every person without missing a chance of speaking aloud my whereabout

My school dress she ironed, tiffin she cooked,

Helpers were many, but she herself did all and arranged  my books,

She took me to the school bus and wished me goodday,

I waved my hands and looked forward to a happy day,

My homework, was her duty more than  mine,

Up to date was my copy with every submission on time,

Days passed by, we all grew up,

My mother grew old, but caring about me she never gave up,

Rich be a mother, poor may be she,

Such a golden heart nowhere else it can be,

A mothers heart knows it all,

How to make her children stand erect and tall,

Not all children are lucky to have their mother,

They are loved and taken care by others,

To respect our mother and to love her is our duty,

To love our parents creates all the beauty,

Not  whole life will our mother be beside us,

Let her blessing be our light that shines always bright enough to guide us.

# 6

## A COBBLER'S TALE

The cobbler mends our shoes,
Did we ever wonder how?
Then run their lives with worries and woes,
Our torn slippers are stitched too good,
Did we ever want to know?
If  he had enough clothes and they had enough food
Shining do our boots emerge, with no signs of dirt,
Did we ever have time to think?
There was neither any shine in their skin, nor was it on their shirt,
He also repaired some  of their high heels,
 Did  we ever  ask ourselves?
How he would feed so many mouths and how did his family feel ?
He had no mobile to receive their orders,
Did we know how he managed?
He worked harder, for more responsibilities to shoulder,
Today Sitaram got his daughters married,
Did we realize how time passed?
He still loves his tool box that he always carried
Our cobbler still mends our shoes so fine,
Did we ever pray?
Let their be dignity of labour, let his efforts also shine!

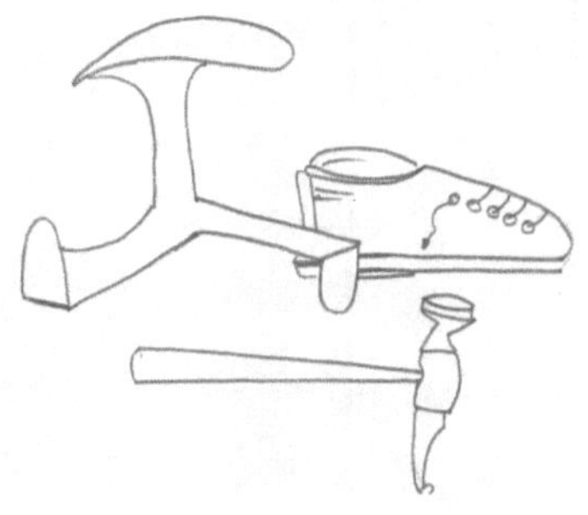

# 7

## FRUIT SALAD

So many fruits, red green and yellow
An apple a day keeps healthy every fellow,
Orange is a rich source of vitamin you see,
Pear you would love to eat whatever the weather be
Guava tastes sweet and banana all likes,
Of all grapes and pomegranate steal the show
How about putting all fruits together ?

Just as fruits are different , so are people,
All are unique whether single or already a couple,
Salad looks so colourful and bright,
Same feel many people, when together they all feel right,
When many fruits are mixed on the plates
No fruit is singly praised, it's the combination that gains the  attention,
How about enjoying the fruit salad all together?

Kiwis are rare, so are avocado,
When you need some shakes , you always remember a mango
Sugarcane is so chilling, so is pineapple,
Watermelons are wonderful, enjoyed lots by many people,
A brilliantly attractive and nutritious a fruit salad appears,
Let us unite as mankind and all our sorrows are sure to disappear.
How about preparing a fruit salad?

# 8

## POSSIBILITIES ARE INFINITE!

Possibilities are infinite ,may be opportunities are rare,

A sapling grows into a tree, life gives chances to all enough fair.

A dream leads to making efforts, which opens up many path

 We select to proceed or not depending on what we get- happy terms or wrath

A lane may singly begin and may bluntly end,

Or may lead to many other paths, to where our imaginations end

Moving ahead has always been an art,

Taking risks require a daring heart,

Options we select, doors we open,

From where comes luck we wonder often,

Work and luck behave like friends hand in hand,

They may also not be together always like a magic wand,

Roads are many but targets are few

Perspiration will ring results with colours and hue.

Not all get opportunities, but possibilities are still present,

We have to work for and wait for good chances and opportunities to befriend!

# 9

## A WHITE COPY

Fresh it looked, with no words or letters in it,

No ink, no line or a name was there to read,

I took out my pen and wrote down my name,

It was in blue, at first it all felt same.

Then came a thought, that I would write  down here my daily activities

But  soon came lockdown, time was more spend with DVDS

It seemed that the copy stared at me with supposedly no further use,

I sat down to paint with red, pink and turquoise,

The next day,I wrote down how went my confined days in home,

I also did some economic calculations,statistical solutions were also done.

Soon my white copy became so useful,

With paintings ,numbers and words, it seemed so gleeful

A white copy it was initially in the beginning,

Now a copy with many information, it became so reasoning,

So our lives are just like a copy so white

Our deeds will add value to it and set it all right !

# 10

## A BOOK AND A CUP

Evening time, street lights lit up the road,

There was slight drizzles,books inside occupied the cupboard;

I sat down  at the table, brought out a wonderful book,

I stretched out my legs,peeped out of the window to have a look

Relaxing in an easy chair there came a cup of tea,

Sip by sip I took and let my thoughts wander whatever it might be,

A cup of coffee would have worked wonders, or may be some ice cream,

One cup of milkshake and a cake would we every ones's dream,

Reading books by the window panes, with rain drops falling by,

No price however much one pays, such comfort one can never buy!

Page after page I turned, and everything seemed to have come to a pause,

This blissful evening was full of magic, you don't need to find a cause!!

Reading the book took away my grief, rains added to my happiness

A good book and a warm cup is enough for one to find some peace !!

# 11

## HER SLING BAG

Her  earrings were dazzling and her duppatta flying by,

She was carrying a stylish sling bag and planning what else to buy

It was brown in colour,with pockets so many,

Having so many bags at home, she mostly selected this bag without missing any,

She put in some money, also she put in her pen,

Also she had her i- card, mobile and carried it everywhere she went,

Her sling bags she liked them enough,

She had about a dozen, selecting any single one was always so tough!

It  looked good with all kinds of dresses ,

It was suitable to carry whether in office or in the printing press,

Foreign trips also she enjoyed carrying her sling bag,

So it did become a part of her outfit,and it was indeed her favourite bag.

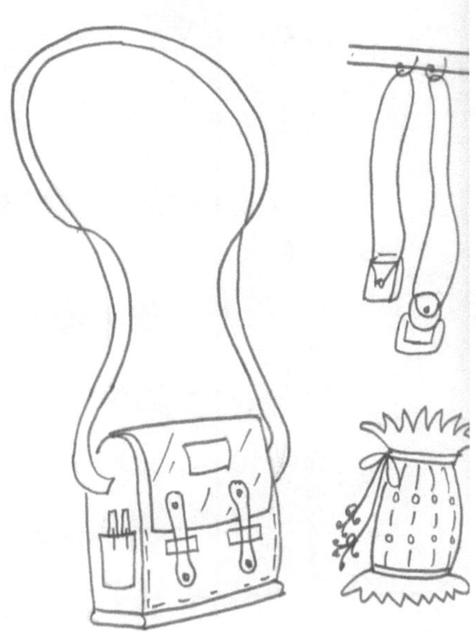

# 12

## THE PASSIONATE PROFESSION

He wanted to be a dancer,

    dance was what he loved,

Some wanted to paint picture,

    through paintings their efforts were proved,

Being a banker was his dream,

    he did not know where to begin,

Technical lines were her fascination,

    she would be happy all by imagination,

Medical fields drew his attention,

    risk required created some tension

Becoming a lawyer, was his prayer,

    books were all over, also in his tables drawer

Cricket was his heartbeat,

    field was his aim

Acting was his passion,

    wanting name and fame

Teachers are known to be sculptures

    of future to be dear,

Singers are perfectionist with knowledge

    of music and instrument all so clear!

Soldiers are praised,

    Army, navy, airforce,

All professions are perfect,

    With bright and beautiful every course

Dignity of labour is

    to be respected obviously,

All men deserve honour

    irrespective of his profession definitely !!

# 13

## THE P.C.O. – THAT WENT MISSING

It stood erect with pride occupying a space so important

The P.C.P it was called , it has now become extinct

Glasses covered it from all sides, one single person it allowed to enter

It was every ones necessity and for many it served for problems that were very tender

News good or news bad, were mostly shared from within it

Continuously was the phone transmitting all information without knowing anything about it

How meager did it cost per call ,we all can be surprised

When no one had a mobile phone to stay connected

Calls national or calls overseas , near or far

Every one was dependent on the P.C.O  it was very clear

 Incessant rain or scorching heat be there,

P.C.O booth stood stout in almost every road's corner

Days have changed , threes have withered

P.C.O are now missing with no phone tethered.

# 14

## HEMIPLAGIA

Hemiplagia is a term so medical

It is a condition all so very critical

Half of the body from top to bottom

Has lost all activities and senses for so long

Only the man survives by his active side

The normal half is the reason that  he is alive

But still he moves forward and tries to walk

With circumduction and Bell's palsy he still tries to talk !

Did you wonder where lies the defect ?

Yes brains or central nervous system is the main culprit

Risk factors are many, some of them are common,

Causes that precipitate are still responsible for dangers they summon.


A country like this man can also be hemiplegic

One  half being formed by the army so gallant

Teachers so hard working and doctors so valiant !

Farmers are toiling, engineeres smartly shining

They form the energetic side of the mankind so appealing

But like a silhouette  so unseen

Lies many lies everywhere to begin

There is corruption and there is back stabbing

And terrorism is there in many regions.

Poverty, robbery and activities of vice

If all these are not removed how will a country rise ?

With one half formed by the progressive fraction,

And other half being the regressive section

How can a country proceed rapidly?

It  has to step forward very cautiously

Risk factors like bad habits are not properly dealt with

Causes like improper character are very difficult to proceed with

 The cure is none or the cure is one

To serve the nation with a devoted heart and moral values as one

# 15

## DANCES OF INDIA

Kathak dance has its glory unquestioned from all times

Do you want to know about its taal ?

Manipuri dance has its special decency in every magnificent sphere

Do you want t o learn about its mudras ?

Kathakali dance spreads its immense charm over the excited audience

Have  you ever tried learning the laya ?

Bharatnatyam so divine, draws all attention

Do you know how beautiful are all the nine rasas?

Kuchipudi dance form is known to have overwhelmed people from time unknown

Do you wonder what is a tarana ?

Odissi  nritya is elegant , every dignified dancer loves this form so well

Have you never wondered about what is a tihai ?

Kshatriya dance so gorgeous makes many eyes to be surprised

Do you not want to know what is som?

Bihu dance is so energetic that people forget their worries and dance to the beats

Have you learnt what is a paran ?

Rabindra nritya remembers Tagore in the sogs written so well

So does ghumar has its lovely dance groups

Garba is a magical dance in all festive to come

Mohiniyattam is a dance form so pure

Dance is indeed the music of our soul and that is for sure!

# 16

## THE PERFECT PARTNER

Surprised will be every soul

Who lives with or without a definite goal

A partner in love, a partner in crime

Is something every man  has desired for a very long time

A friend he is or a friend he is not

Doesn't define the quiescent qualities he got

Some teach us some team spirit may be,

Others help us make a good cup of tea


I might learn how to be helpful

And you might love always to be grateful

A schoolmate or a batch mate he may be

Sitting by the side with a common urge to feel free

None of us are good enough to be perfect

But we can try our level best to do everything right

A true partner if we can become in someone's need

 A new friend is undoubtedly gained indeed

Rarely in a lifetime we get that perfect one

Chance to share with him every thought and all the stuff that is done

Perfect partner is all that we seemingly desire

We believe that all partners are perfect that makes life less bizarre !

# 17

## ON A LIGHTER NOTE

Friend we want, about friend do we care

Did we ever wonder, that we may be left with no friends to share

Mobile phones are an necessity, I would never say no,

Without it I wonder where the whole world would go?

Laptops are our friends as long as our eyes would allow

So are televisions for many to enjoy the show

 But a call and some chat can make our day,

In no way a video game player would feel the similar way

Gadgets are our needs, no doubt about that,

True friends are earned by our deeds, ask our heart about that!

A gloomy day,a heavy heart, a teary eye will always search,

A warm hug and a friends shoulder, I pray there is no dearth.

Type in mobiles save in laptops, play video games,

In the mean time  also remember some good friends name

A day will come when we will only think

How beautiful a life with friends was over as if in a blink !!

# 18

## A PATRIOT IN EVERY HOME

Every heart has a country, every home has a patriot,

May be he walks on foot, or maybe he rides a chariot.

Often I say long live my country, often I sing a song for her,

Every heart has a country, every home has a patriot

Tricolor paints our lives, helps us all stand erect,

Our hearts always sing the song, trying to sound all so perfect,

Tears in our eyes and with inflated chest

We stand together, trying to do our best

Long live India,long live our countrymen,

Facing all challenges and bringing all high achievements.

Every mother is a teacher, every child holds a future,

Every person has a patriot in him and realizing that we feel much better

Every border, every job, every work and every dream

Our country makes a patriot, everyday in every stream

# 19

# THE BANKS OF THE RIVER BARAK

Mighty stands the Sadarghat bridge,

        welcome to Silchar does it say.

Peacefully flows river Barak

        ,important it  is in every way.

Banks of the river are guarded

        by high surrounding embankments

Protected feels the Silchar town,

        protected are her peoples' enhancements,

From the town area,

        when we move towards the remote villages,

Embankments are roughly maintained ,

        so we have to move some extra mileages ,

Diving in the river to bathe,

        also some people for boating to go,

Fishing is someone's profession,

        if not here then where else to go!

Safe be the people bathing,

        safe be the fishermen,

 High tides have some warning protocols

        , followed safely by all men

Peoples main water source

        it is from olden times,

By the banks of river Barak were born many brave hearts,

        names written in history's golden lines.

Many tributaries are distributed,

        forming a meshwork all around.

Clothes of villagers drying nearby

              move with winds making noise and sound.

Colleges of Medical ,Engineering, Polytechnique,

              Law and University stands  upright

Railway station, tea estates, airport,

              many other developments, glorify her insight

Ranges of Khasia hills and

              bold Borail hills on one bank do stand

On  the other bank is Manipur, Mizo

              Tripura hills forming an elongated band.

Field sof paddy, wheat and rice

              are spread across miles,

On the bank of river barak

              do many people stand and smile

# 20

## PEARLS AND ERRORS

Errors like straw on water shall flow,

Those who want true pearls, shall dive into the water below

Drawbacks are conjuring one by one

Perfectionism is something no one cares for, but it will surely cure everyone

Critics feel good, learners feel fooled,

Learned behave miserly and some illiterate luminaries feel so thrilled

Shadows are discussed., images edited

Characters are assassinated , few persons are forever deleted

Light is too shiny for those who remove their long worn sunglasses

Darkness is so deep , it doesn't seem to end over those tall grasses

Let the awakening of our conscience illuminate our minds,

Let the brighter side be focused to heal the mankind

Qualities are to be revealed for sure

Minor misdeeds overlooked may bring the cure

Take time to know the truth and then analyze every detail

Life will surely bring us to a point where we can witness the inauguration of a perfect tale

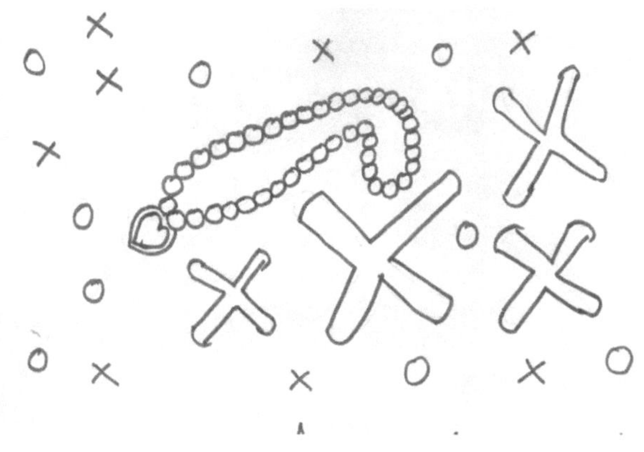

# 21

## THE GIRL WITH A RED UMBRELLA

The rain drops fell from the sky and no one would ask why

It splattered all over her red umbrella, making her tears feel so shy

She was standing on the sea shore

No one disturbed her and she enjoyed the scenery like never before

A beautiful frock she was wearing and also two plain slippers,

Evening was hovering and the darkness grew deeper.

Gradually as she was relaxed ,walking in the rain

 Her emotions took their turns to torment her brain,

Away she lowered her umbrella by the side,

Drenched she was all over with no one to stand beside

The rain water washed away her grief

She wondered if there was any reason to ponder in brief!

Her good memories helped her overcome the difficult times she reckoned

She felt happy as a flourishing future from far was all that in her life beckoned

The girl with a red umbrella now started to smile

The rain by the sea shore ,washed away all her reasons to whine.

# 22

## INSOMNIA

A peaceful  night's sleep is what all people want

But is it so easy to own the blessing?

Some have night shifts and some have ailing family members to attend,

Is it possible for us to avoid the compulsory duties entrusted at night?

Even in a bed so cosy ,some lay awake for hours

Do we know what can be the underlying cause?

Some might have experienced a heartbreak, others may have some stressful situation

Can we help them to calm down a little?

Some students worry a out their exams , some old men still complain of lack of sleep

Do we have better ways to deal with this ?

Medications are many , counseling sessions are there too

But are we open minded or unprejudiced to them ?

A rich man's sleep or poor man's be it

Everyone has right to sleep for long hours at night

A healthy mind resides in a healthy body

A sound sleep is sure to make you mentally wealthier

Insomnia ! insomnia !! insomnia !!!

Be benevolent, scientific and tolerant, sleep will soon follow like panacea!

# 23

# THE TAKE OFF

Journeys are fascinating, travelling seems magical

Boarding on an aeroplane was  was everyones desire since childhood

And so were hidden vacations in store

An air travel and a holiday package, what can one ask for more?

People  of all ages went for their luggage checking

One after another travelers stood in a long queue

Happiness was in  every heart,soon they would be flying , that's all that they knew

All  boarding passes received and all handbags were tagged

Forward they moved towards their seats with the excitement they never lacked

Fastened were their seat belts , straightened were their seats

Many put their i-pod's earphones and moved their heads with the music beats

It was the time to take off, with pilots voice floating

Air hostesses gave their demonstration and this diversion prevented unnecessary bloating

Some prayed with immense devotion ,some held tightly their seat handles

The mobile phones were  switched off and the old man searched for his pair of sandals

Their grip tightened , eyes widened and breathing became deep

Soon the flight took off and everyone breathed a sigh of relief

Up into the sky at last the plane was seen flying

All with a lighter heart enjoyed the journey and thereafter kept smiling.

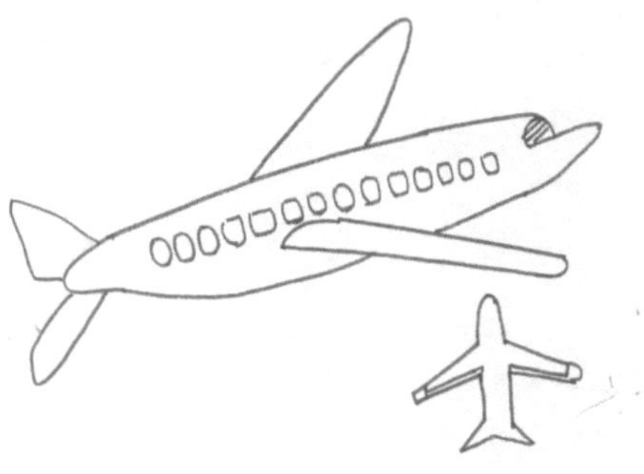

# 24

## SPIRIT

Poetic thoughts are many that often intrigues our glistening minds,

To which thought to respond is unclear to us, we may not be all of the same kind

Ambitions soar high, incidents happen by, what should we explain to someone

Who also say coincident happen simultaneously in parallel universe of a happy man

Not knowing the vehement values of goodness if one proceeds,

In no way one with a sickeningly selfish heart can truly succeed

Ink and paper can shapes almost everyone's future

What we become is merely a reflection of our character

Sometimes appropriate words may me we what we can fall short of

Not knowing what our feelings mean when lights are turned off

A heart that is true will always find a way to you

Irrespective of the difficult consequences or differences that were not very few

The heart with blazing love cannot go hidden

The strength of true love could never be forbidden

A mother ,father, life partner or sibling he or she may be

A spirit so fearless like them have the courage to always surrender to Thee.

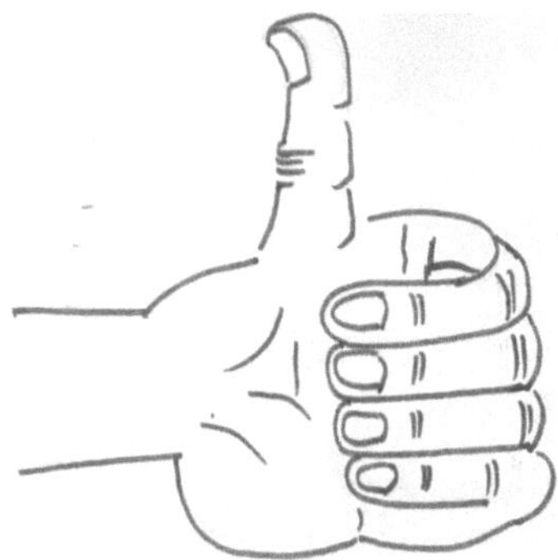

# 25

# DEMENTIA – GOOD OR BAD ?

You hate yourself if you forget something

Your boss dislikes you if you forget a simple thing

But  do you realize the advantage of not remembering certain stuff ?

Like if you don't let your memory carry the glimpses of a day that was full of insult

Or  may be some unintentional action that made you cry in guilt.

Rightly said some one that you forget things if you  don't want to remember them

But  with memories sharp and being able to recollect old incidents

Remembering infrequently seen faces are qualities always defined to be decent

It is indeed a boon for student's academic curriculum to say

But forgetting some unlucky happening is also good in a way

Time heals the mental trauma , also teaches the nature

Forgetting some undesired past is a beautiful part of our brain's feature

God forbid any accident or disease to affect the memory of a person

Dementia of old age is an important liability of any young daughter or son

When children forget to do their homework

Parents and teachers look into the matter to find out what teaching skills would still work

Inspite of having willingly forgotten or undesired state of ill health had fallen

Forgetting is not welcome for all people whose fruits of  thoughts have now ripened

We should try to get all our duties done

And forgetfulness should not be an excuse for leaving things undone

# 26

## THE MALLS STAND TALL

Villages are vanishing with rapid urbanization

Cities are adorned with malls beyond all expectations

Towns are lucky to acquire the golden opportunity

But the occupants of the demolished areas are shifted to places with not much priority


Malls stand tall with merchandise so huge

All living an ecstatic life going out and shopping with family

But at the shadow of the staircase are some people with gloomy face

Who try to sell some balloons, beg or do things for their own poverty's ache


Light I have focused, so also lurks and peeps in some penumbra

Asset is any mall for a small town or a city very big

But their people are also the potential human resource forming a country's vertebra

Happy are all when inside a mall,

Food courts are full of hustle and bustle


Games are played , movies enjoyed

So many people got new jobs and all of them were well paid

But grim clouds hovered all of a sudden, without any warning

Lockdown affected all people and spoilt the atmosphere so charming

It persisted for a few months and every one prayed

Believing that every cloud has a silver lining , as wise men of all times have said

MALL
BIG MARKET
KCF
DIMONOS
VIKAL
PEP

# 27

## LOVE LETTERS THAT MATTER

From school days and from movie songs
All student also learn little about love letters and some try to write along

With nothing to understand, and feel so deeply
Teenagers write love letter with many mistakes done unknowingly,

Some write a poem, others may write an essay,
Trying to please him or her in a special way

Many a times parents and teachers tear such letters,
But young children will hide them to attempt to read them later

Growing up they will judge things so wisely
That the fragrance of these early emotions become clear very slowly

They now think and rethink before sitting down to write one
Love letters to his or her extra special one

Whether things lead to marriage or not is not the matter
What actually happens is these epistle always reveal something innocent to share

Feelings true from heart are penned down, that also include some random thoughts
Some letters indeed fulfill the purpose that those writings have always sought !

# 28

## A MAID WHO SMILED

There was once a maid whose story is known to many,
Good she was by nature,would do many extra work without any extra penny.
Cleaning the floors and the school walls was her duty
She never felt shy and caringly did her work with all beauty

Many students came to the school and went, creating many success stories
 Her life remained all the same with only full of worries
Gradually her work was well rewarded , her son became a graduate
Soon her wrinkles seemed to smoothen and her facial expressions illuminate

A teacher of the school where she worked, with time her son became
This was the happiest time in her life that slowly came
A maid she was earlier, a lady she is now
Her son made her dreams come true, spreading smiles anyhow !

# 29

## AS THE HAIR TURNS GREY

When you have bidden farewell to the spring season in your life

When you feel that life's winter is nearing and you are reading a newspaper with your wife

Your bones seemed to have weakened and hair has turned grey

 You still feel your inner self is young in all possible way

Your body feels mortal, subject to not so blissful aging

Your heart aches to comprehend the reality, that your body will soon start aching


The men do colour their moustache and beard

The women colour their hair and listen to songs they have already heard

Sometimes by fluke grey hairs are seen shining and at times their eyes twinkle

All beauty is gradually lost with some creeping wrinkle

Many lessons learned , many seasons lived,

Much happiness enjoyed and some sadness grieved


Memories are only that remains with faces so hazy

Spectacles and sticks are their new company , yet they feel so lazy

Children have grown up, with most duties done

Grandchildren started going to schools with some homework still left undone

Life's autumn has set in and its winter shall follow

Enjoy every moment and till death love every fellow !

# 30

## A PRINCESS FROM A FAR AWAY LAND

Once upon a time there was one King and his Queen indeed;

Do you know what their story was about?

They had a little princess who learnt martial arts so splendid !

Yes she would practice with gleeful cheers and shout,

They had the fear of their enemy's plans to attack them !

And one night  their fears turned true and scary!

They had a very short time and the princess was their only hope then,

She formed an army,and proved to be very daring!

Fierce was the fight, lives were lost,women were widowed and children orphaned

She fought in a way so gallant, forgetting that she had a little chance,

But men, women and children all left their houses and with the army they joined !

Her chances to win became double , happiness made her to think to dance,

Under  the King, Queen , and bold princess' authority,

Did the countrymen put their lives and heart together!

Standing together through thick and thin,they all won their country's victory

Hence the princess saved her country , with no one else to bother !

# 31

## CHILDHOOD CHOCOALATES

Little did we know, how fast shall we grow

Studying with mother or playing with father

With toys and books did pass our days,

Friends and siblings created memories in many ways.

Kitkat, Cadbury's, gems and milkibar are the names of few,

Munch, nutties ,chewing gums and many more came out  so new

Simple were our wishes, though we could not make our favourite dishes,

Now that we can cook, we rarely find some time to read a new book,

Not  all children see the comfort, schools and pretty tennis court

We must pray for them, share a meal, and spread some smiles with a helping hand.

Small deeds can touch their hearts and change their day as if with a magic wand,

Smile is a spark when seen on one face,

When many wil smile together, it shall set all grief ablaze.

Cloth, food and sweets , a fair share shall we do

Little did we know how fast shall we grow !!

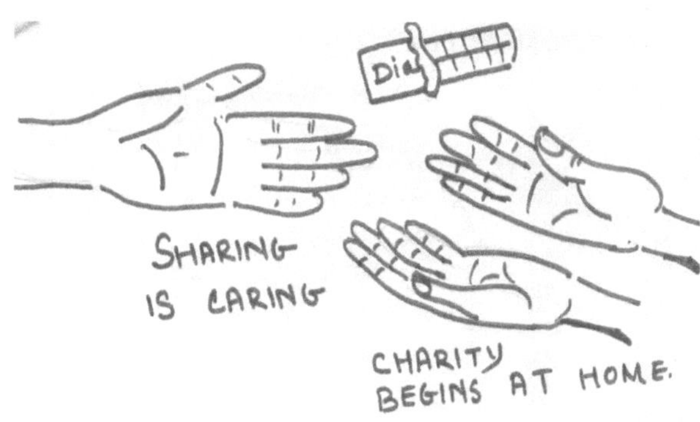

# 32

## THE SHOW CASE

Stood there a wonderful showcase,

With varied things beautifully kept in different place


Of  shiny wood was its body carpentered from,

Also painted wonderfully with bright colours out of norm.


Its door were made of glasses,

Inside were kept many cups and dishes.


So were kept many prizes they won,

The big and small metal statues in the light they shone,


Also there were kept many toys and dolls,

I wonder how their childhood tossed in a roll!


Paintings hanging nearby were so neat

The arist was an expert, his works one cannot easily beat.


In the showcase were some childhood pictures

Also of family members ,made emotions develop of awesome mixture!


Stood there a wonderful showcase,

With varied things beautifully kept in different place

# 33

## THE NON RESIDENTS

Home and heart go side by side,

The non residents may have some rules to abide,

Emotions are separate, you miss your mother –tongue,

Languages may be different but workplaces are proudly sung

Unity in diversity shall all celebrate,

Variations in individual lives , no one shall begin a debate,

Some need documents to prove, some need to buy some land,

We all began as a cell and shall die in ashes or sand,

Wherever shall we be, we should have a heart all so great,

To love our workplace and also the place of ancestors where our memories began to generate

States may be different, countries may vary,

Love and respect for both places if intact, there is no reason to worry

Enjoy  the optimism and shrug away the separation,

Wipe away all tears, let smiles lead to celebration

# 34

## BUCKET LIST

She had a long list, also similar had he,

List of things to do and places where to be !

Some wanted to go to Paris, some wanted to ride a ship,

Going to a mall was a dream for many,as they could only buy clothes so cheap.

Some desired to go for sky diving, some wanted to play guitar

She wanted to do Bungee jumping, her children wanted to play sitar !

She wanted to spend a night in the Arctic

Some only desired to built a cosy bed in the attic.

To keep a horse as a pet and riding it was in her list,

To touch a dolphin and play with it was what he wanted in a jist!

She planned to read a hundred books , all in only one weeks time,

He cooked a variety of delicious dishes only for his wife to dine

Some still wish to go to school, some still want to drink safe water,

We must try in every way to make our countrymen feel better!

Things to do are listed in ways so plenty,

May God fulfil everyones wishes and may he bless in bounty.

# 35

# THE PHOTOFRAME

Long back did she leave us, but in the photo she still smiles,

This is the charm of a photoframe, which grabs a moment from uncountable miles,

Our childhood days were captured and so were some seconds of many occasions,

Our grandparents bless us through photoframes and help us  to take many life decisions.

It stole a smile from my youth, it was sweet , a smile so bright,

I see the difference, compare and feel what people say is so right.

Generation after generation, photoframe swill work  like wonder,

Preserving the family's pictures, and compelling time to somewhat surrender!

Foreign trips' photos  and pictures of  marriages also flaunt the walls

Beautiful landscapes were captured and so were pictures of embroidered hand woven shawls!

The photoframe seems like a portal helping us to travel in time

Keeping safe many moment from past and alive in memories of yours and mine!

# 36

## THE SPARKLING DROP, MADE JAWS DROP

The clouds were grey, wind blew in a soothing way,

The clothes on the terrace moved with the winds in a rhythmic sway;

The little drops from the sky fell on the ground,

Magical was what we heard, rain drops made such a sound

Thunders and bright lightening filled everyone's heart with joy

Puddles and splashes of water filled the heart of every boy!

So the farmers were happy, happy were the umbrella store owners,

Happy were the book lovers ,who read books in some cozy corners

Grew louder the thunder, became heavier the shower,

No one could predict when it would stop, it was beyond our power!

Rivers were swollen, fields were flooded,

Floods were everywhere, everyone seemed stranded

Broken down were some walls, some bridges were carried along,

Cries were heard everywhere, people went to places they did not belong,

Boat surveillance and relief works were started,

Hopes rose high when food was being distributed.

Lasted for a few days this terrible situation,

Saved were some people from despair and oblivion,

At  last all these came to an end,

People rushed to their homes without wasting a second,

Crops were destroyed so were some houses

Some men lost their family members, some lost their spouses.

Rain is welcome but not in this manner

May God forbid such situations to recur!

# 37

## DE NOVO !

The mud so wet,with drops of dew,

The fresh new grass, bright green it grew,

The calf ran fast in fear of a car,

The driver drove slow to save the calf so dear.

The kitten stared and waited for some milk,

The mistress gave her some to drink, wearing a dress made of silk.

A baby crawled there up on the stairs

Surprised was he with the sunlight to glare.

Out came his mother to look for him,

Crawling outside his home now seemed like a dream.

New are little lives with bodies so tiny

Blessed are all those with love so shiny!

The puppy barked at the sight of the child,

He never knew the dangers out their in the wild!

Elders are always known to nurture a big range of affection,

For all so young and beautiful , beyond any definition.

De novo begins life and so it continues,

Every day is a new beginning and an undeterred speed it determines.

# 38

## THE GREEN CURTAINS

In her house so beautiful,curtains were silky green in colour,

Decorations were imported , flowers nice, all seemed very close to nature,

As the days passed by, she started feeling good about her curtains

She loved them a lot and it was indeed very certain

Pets she did have , and she had a well knit family,

Good were her furniture, so were her sets of cutlery

There once came a day, she knew not why, she suffered from immense pain,

She visited a doctor and took all measures, but all the medicines went in vain,

It  was a hospital she had to be taken,

All her family members were no doubt so shaken

In there she started feeling like home, green were the curtains which gave her some relief,

The idea that she would soon go home ,made her happy and she had this belief

An operation was needed and she was cured,

With other medications decreased the pain that she had to endure,

Few days she needed some help, as it was her hospital stay,

But the sight of the hospital curtains that were green made her worries go at bay

At last she was released and her happiness knew no bounds

Her family pleased and she could again hear the city sounds,

She reached her home and saw her curtains were still,

To create a source of happiness is there within evryones will

Curtains green, curtains red,curtains are of every colour,

Hospital stay needs support and care, that is what all need to know very clear.

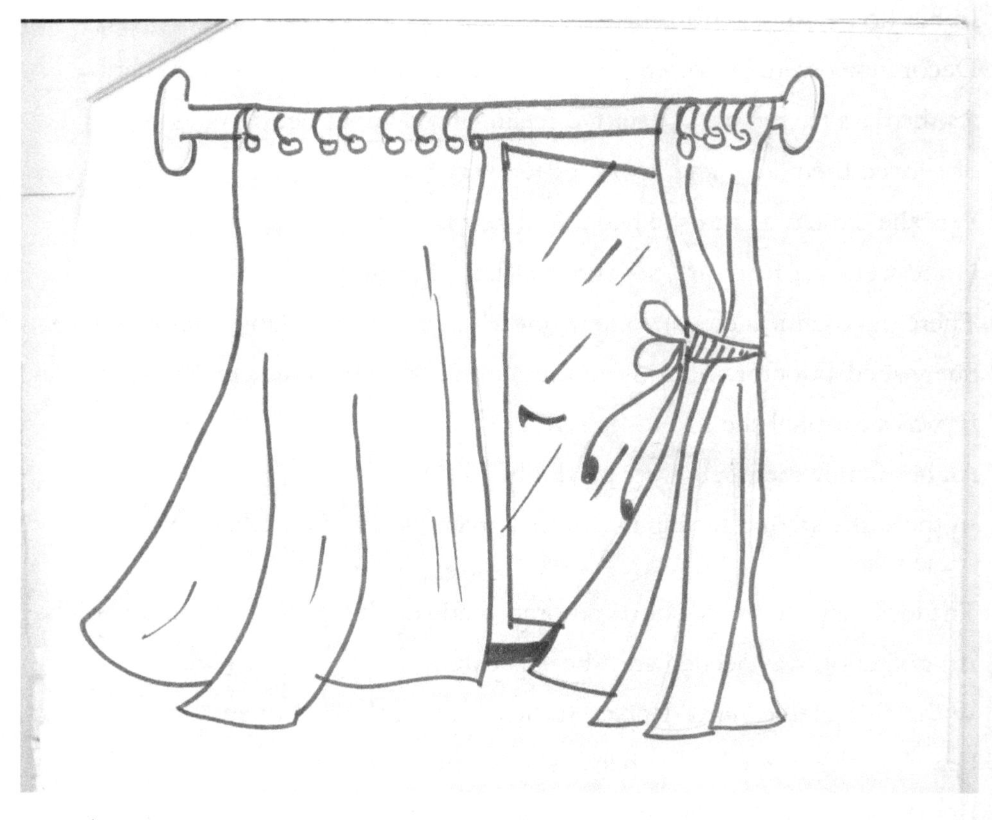

# 39

## GRAND PA !!

With a heart of gold, my tiny hands he would hold.

Sweets he would share and showered me with love and care.

As grew mothers love, so grew his too.

Holding my fingers , for many walks he would go.

Be it our playgrounds or be it our school,

He went there everywhere where parents could not go!

Stories were his strength, be it fiction or mythology,

They made my meals fast and a bit easy.

Fairs he would take me to, marketing he would enjoy,

Nothing could resist him, he did everything for our joy.

If  he was fas, he would write few letters,

Reading them used to make me feel better

Not  for a long time was the company, but pure was the bond,

One night he passed away ,leaving memories so fond.

# 40

## THE SUNNY SIDE

He clapped for my prize, she clapped for me not,

It  didn't much change the value of what I got;

She shared her notes, he stole my paintings,

I learnt what is true and false, I learnt it beyond all bindings.

She was happy for my performance, they were a bit envious,

Not all men are good , some are also dubious.

He listened to her cry and turned back and reached her,

Some said she deserved to wipe her own tears,few people also ditched her!

Some praised her for the running races she won,

Some raised their eyebrows seeing the outfit she worn,

Some respcetd him for his decency,

While others judged his character depending on his earned currency

A lot many said that he can never write a success story

For those who believed him, he came out with shining glory

All are fragile , all are docile, but all have the potential,

The brighter side you focus more, the more it becomes beneficial,

For the one who praised, the one who respected and the one who felt happy

However cloudy life's days may seem, your soul still finds a reason to feel sunny!

# 41

## CUTE COSMETICS

A fine girl she is, good in job and ware,

A good woman she is, with two children to care

Brushed were stroked, colours were blended,

Brighter she looks , her wrinkles were mended,

Red were her lips, blue were her eyelashes,

Bron were her hair, with all pink blushes,

A smile she would carry, which washed away all worry,

Without which all cosmetics seemed a bit blurry,

Cosmetics are cute, a smile cuter,

Happiness of the heart should grow greater,

A lady she was, not properly listened

A women she grew into, whose eyes never glistened,

A face so sweet, with cosmetics look better

Her weeping heart somehow felt bitter!

Coloured be her dreams, happier be her heart

Deeper be her mascara, and closer she be to her sweethearts

# 42

## OUR BIRTHDAYS – MERRY GO ROUND

The day we were born,is what constantly reappears

Year after year we grow unnoticed , and on that day all our sorrows disappear

Like a merry go round , this special day is reached

Many plans are made, many guests invited and time tables are breached

Loud clinks of glasses and splatters of plates are heard

Every guest seems to be treated like a Santa claus without any sledge or beard,

Gifts are treasured , cakes are disturbed

Also other childrens' birthday plans are also stipulated,

Big or small however the celebration might be,

Some children even faced a lockdown birthday party,which sounds so difficult to me,

Someone lights a candle ,some one offers prayers

Some people wait for charity and meals which are still not theirs,

Birthdays are one of the happiest days of the year upcoming,

Let us spread more smiles by becoming more caring

# 43

## THE WINE AND THE LOBSTER

A beautiful lady dressed in red,

Waited for her love to come and join,

She finished her work on time and left her ailing mother in the bed,

She waited still to see his face and alongwith tossed a coin,

He would come or he would not,

Continuously it was what she thought!

A well dressed man with a clear expression,

Entered the room and gave her a smile

He had a decent accent and was full of passion,

Waiting for so long gave her butterflies in her stomach, but she rested for a while,

Seeing him take his seat,

Her face seemed to glow , with no emotion to beat.

They started to laugh and chat

And ordered some red wine and spicy lobster

Deepened were their gaze, and both of them noticed that

Eating and smiling they felt like life is a roller coaster

Delicious was the meal and they started feeling comfortable,

Thinking about spending a life ahead together was finally decided across their table!

# 44

## FALSE FLOWERS VS FRESH BLOOMS

Their garden looked magical, with wonderful sights and scents,

Fresh were those flowers with varied colours,

Adorned were their living room, with decoration so decent,

False were the leaves and flowers spread indoors,

No comparision will stand the test of glory

Between the roses in the garden and those in hand

False flowers gave joy but true blossoms completed the story

We know not where the debate would stand

Prayers needed the real flowers always so dear,

Be it temples, churches or some near ones' grave

Every man has to arrange them from far or near,

To praise the Almighty and adorn the memories of the lost lives of the brave,

May be false datura , sunflowers and daisy made someones' pocket full,

Real marigolds and gajra are used to make garlands so neat,

In a shop the absence of the false flowers made it look so dull,

True blossoms have a charm so true, which no velvet or plastic flowers  can beat

# 45

## THE LAMPS I LIT

Cloudy were the skies,wind was blowing,

The sparkling festival of Diwali was that day, with decorations mind blowing,

Since childhood have we cherished this evening,

Lighting the lamps, diyas and candles gave life its meaning

 Welcoming Lord Rams was what the history says,

Victory of good over evil is what the sound track plays,

A splendid evening full of fireworks and crackers,

 With sweets designed specially made in home and from bakers,

Gifts were exchanged , prayers performed,

And as if in a blink of an eye, we all were transformed,

From children playing all around,

To youth with life partners, and family to surround

New kurtas, lehengas, and with all jewelleries so new

Rangoli was made and they all had some snacks to chew,

Little do we realize that we all will grow old soon,

With family lighting the same lamps since the time we were born

The lamp we lit yesterday , brings memories of joy and hope,

With the light it spread, gave us all a life possible to cope!!!

# 46

## FAR ACROSS THE DISTANCE

Brother he is mine, yet he is so far,

Job it is infact , all so indispensible,

Friends were so dear,we enjoyed each  others company,

But time came when we all were spread far apart,

Distance became so intervening, and yet accepted as normal,

We never knew how our relations soon turned so digital!

Phone calls, skype, wassap is all that we like

Facebook, twitter, instagram is all that we get used to so often,

Going to playgrounds or visiting kith and keen , is what now so rare to be seen,

Sisters meet after ages, parents and children are in different countries,

Widespread are our family and friends,

Yet so dearly we feel their presence within our hearts,

 Far across the distance is about what every heart thinks of before falling into a deep slumber,

This is how time flows by from January to December.

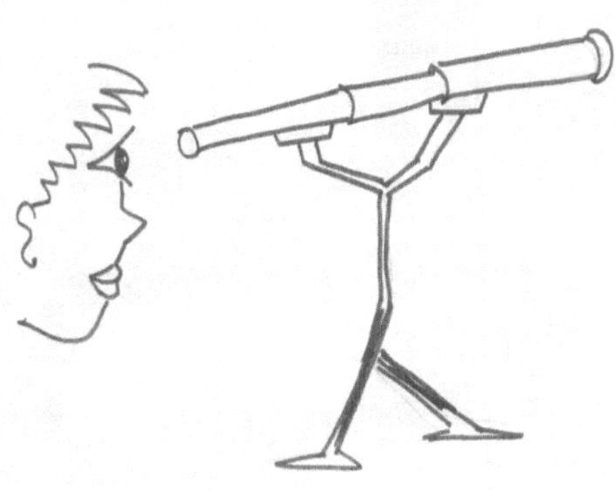

# 47

## 31ST DECEMBER

Year ending has arrived, hip hip hurray!
A new beginning is about to start, happiness is on its way

All are waiting for the clock to strike 12 AM
People all over the world will celebrate it like a dream

Some over the television will commemorate
Some will enjoy in a party

Others will spend their night in a beach
To applaud and sing till they witness a sunshine so bright

Another year has already passed with many different stories
Every life on earth always adds to her glory

To welcome a new year has always been the tradition
Burning crackers offering prayers becomes the fascination

A new year is awaiting , so are our plans,
We also indulge in music , good food , drinks and some dance

Soon it shall all be over with lingering charm to hover
As the the new year begins , restarts the  pursuit of  a new chapter to discover

HAPPY
NEW YEAR

# 48

## THE KEY WE SEARCH FOR

We all want our wishes to be granted

All problems vanquished like our forefathers always wanted

Our imaginations to become realities ,our desires to get fulfilled

Destinations reached on time and to –do list accomplished,

But did we ever think how will all these be ever possible

Without a key of magic enough to solve mysteries intangible

All locks need a key, without which it is a pity

But  till today we are in voracious search of that selected key

Taking initiatives, beginning actions and toiling for what we want

Can definitely unlock all the secrets and help us make all get stunned

 Hard work and perspiration, logical approach and some preparation

Is what the key is made up of , should be consciously known to all the generation

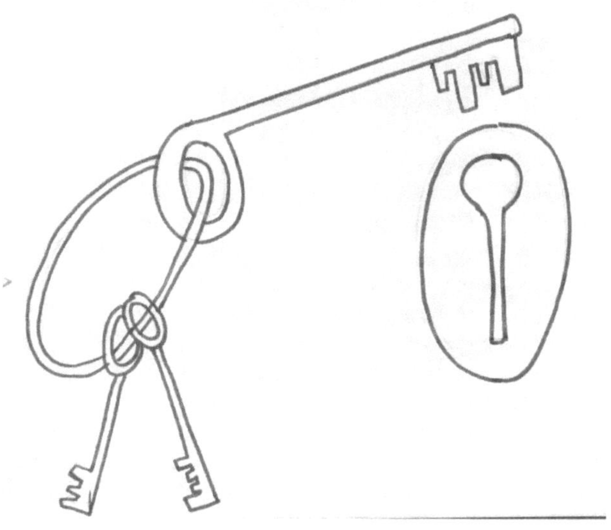

# 49

## EMOTIONAL ENZYME

Whet the boss shouted you heard that with all your mind,

Upon you is bestowed natures' bliss to hold the soul divine

Criticisms are narrations of ones own desperation,

If not balanced , this can generate the process of destruction,

Enthusiasm is the need of the solemnly wild hour,

You need to swallow all despair and do yourself a favor,

Anger and rage has ruined all ages,

If you do not control it, it may curb your wages,

If we cant digest food, enzymes solve our problem,

Similarly , a little bit of tolerance can do all miracles,

Solace, calmness and steadiness is all that we need,

However small or great may appear our deed,

Emotions are deep rooted , emotions are volatile

Dealing with them carefully will no doubt make ourselves docile.

# 50

## THE BOTTLE AND THE CIGARETTE

He sat by the balcony's edge, drinking beverages from the bottle

As it became empty , he felt as if his emotions rushed towards him to throttle

The empty bottle was of no use to him

He lit a cigarette and his convictions changed sides at the verandas brim.

He let his thoughts wander hither and thither

He undoubtedly started  enjoying this charm on an evening in winter

One after another five cigarettes did he smoke,

He cursed his habits for all the harms he had evoked

His lungs craved for some fresh air,

His mind gave him certain  ideas very dear

To take the bottle that was empty,

And fill it with happy and treasured experiences  even if  they were scanty

As every day gives us a reason to smile

And that is what we need to pen down,

Writing in small chits each day about some  memorable moments,

And filling up the bottle with some paper pieces without any rough comments,

The number of cigarettes gradually started  counting less,

Full was the bottle soon with many mesmerizing memories to bless.

# 51

## GOOD CHAIN

Bad habits die hard

Good habits are difficult to develop

Good begets good generally

Who knows what's in an envelope?

It may have a letter with warm wishes

It may bring in some blessing as cash

Or it may carry an order from a senior officer

But in no way it is supposed to be harsh

One act of kindness draws attention

With many hands together someones's feelings can strengthen

A smile can pass on to a crowd

A chain of good things can always lengthen

One candle can light the second

What is important is the power to begin

Spreading it will be welcome

Energy budding from everywhere can be seen

Good chains if practiced in corporate sector

Brain drain will get curtailed like malaria vector

Grey matter within our country will get better chance

One does not need to travel to The U.K.or to  France

Chains of action , marketing or fun may be

Sharing books , food or clothes may be

A good chain will no doubt bring a change

In a good world we can improve in whichever way it might be

# 52

## HAPPINESS !!

Happiness is in contentment, so do many say,
What exactly is happiness? All explanations will stay at bay!

A child is happy to get the toys he wants
He is happy to eat the toffee he sees

All men want fame , that is where lies the secret
Some man look good and act, some men play cricket

The needy want some discount or charity
The student before exams want to think with clarity

The pursuit of happiness is never ending
Within home or abroad one needs sharing

Human wants are generally not limited
But the state of happiness need not be intimidated

Blessed are those who feel happy from within
Rich are they by soul who can smile whatever situation they are in

We all are humans with time so short
Happy should we be, or else we not have anything to fight for

# 53

## PERICARDIUM

The outer covering of heart is called pericardium
I wish our feelings similarly had a protective pericardium

Biologically a pericardium is all so very important
Emotionally it even doesn't exist as if it wanted our heart to feel the torment

Words spoken are the means to either conceal or express
The feelings that are happy or that make you feel depressed

With no pericardium, our emotions are vulnerable and naïve
Be very selective of people as you have a sensitive emotional heart to save

However wise you might seem, Fate plays the final role
Bound are you by your deeds, so pretty knows your soul

Through prayers and actions you may try to purify
Like the outer covering of the heart good deeds will create results that can glorify

Be good and do good and the rest will follow
His heart may have vibes very deep or may be very shallow

Pericardium may at times develop inflammation
Likewise not hurting others or yourself should be your determination

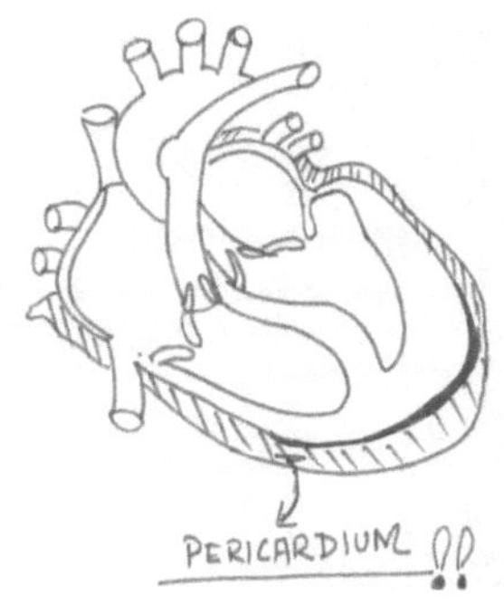

# 54

## A GAME OF CHESS

A brilliant game is chess of all known times
You may have learnt techniques learnt from  your family or friends of mine

Kings, Queens and horses are all  nearly ready
At the perfect hour , the game should become steady

A war as if on the boards is being fought
 With minds ad sharpness the points are being sought

Life is too like a game of chess
Level after level you understand all the mess

The attack is on and the game is active
 Sometimes the results of the game are not predictive

The black and white party plays their part
With alternate boxes does the player feel very smart

Beautifully generated are the rules of the game
If you cannot appreciate it, its such a shame

A game of chess is so interesting
A feeling of challenge it always does bring
Checkmate is the word one player waits to utter
The winner should show sportsman's spirit and let not his opponent shudder

# 55

## ONE WHO TOPS THE LIST

Lucky and deserving candidate he is

Highest are his scores and the first rank goes to him

Others need not loose hopes so fast as

The other positions still remain with all scopes not so dim

Stands first his brother in science

Open remains other subjects for another

Games and sports are also very promising

A little efforts and worries will be diminishing

Stubborn for success those who become

If not tops in  the first  list, surely will top in the second

Rest lies in endeavor and endurance

No one can predict the future it comes with no assurance

Disheartened should not be the runners up

Participation indeed is also to applaud for the winners' cup

Had there been no audience ever

Games and  culture  would have made histories never

There is a place for all no doubt

Keep up practicing your trials constanly, silently or aloud!

# 56

# PROBLEMS AND PROBLEMS !!

Problem is a term common to me and you

Every situation today or tomorrow presents it to all of us too


We can all afford problems, but solutions are priceless

Elated are those who on the real and possible solutions can focus


Some have visited  the Niagara falls , some might have started at the ranges of the Himalayas

Problems do each one of us come across whether staying in New York, India, or LasVegas


A child has a mathematical problem , a youth has something emotional,

As long as we don't overcome the problems, we cannot become developmental


An old man sees the beckoning problems of death and afterlife

Little does he know, who will die earlier, either he or his beloved wife


Political, vocational, economical problems lie everywhere

Inspite of all these we have to make progress, or else we will lead to nowhere


Problems yesterday, problems today, problems tomorrow will always be there

Finding a way out and moving ahead is our motto as if in life's fastest gear !

# 57

## SCHOOL DAYS !

Long ago we left behind a station in the journey of our lives
The train of life whistles and we turn back to realize how fast time flies

Hazy memories , clear faces, crazy incidents,
                all present to us at once as if alive in a flash
Few seconds ago I remembered who is my best friend
                and with whom I had some clash.

Competition fair, friendship lively were the assets of our school days
Apart from proper and classic academics, we learnt in various ways

Games were played, poems recited, exams we appeared,
Prizes were won, lectures attended and soon we grew up and disappeared .

Teachers played an enormous role in bringing us up
English,Mathematics, Science and Arts we always knew how to keep it up

Today our school helps us remember the child within us
Cherish prayerfully each day of your school, soon you will  be out for years

Thanks to all the people who help us become educated
Long live our schools, may their students always win and remain undefeated .

# 58

## DO YOU LOVE ME ? – A MILLION DOLLAR QUESTION

The children in the orphanage, the widow who will remarry

All have the same question on love, as its about their life that they will carry!


The patients in the hospitals, aged people in the old care homes,

Want to know if people still do love them genuinely even after their duty is done


The plants and trees around us and all over are so helpful

Do we love their existence ,which is of utmost importance and indeed very needful


The animals on the road are so scared of the running vehicles.

We should be careful enough not to harm them whether physical or chemical


Do you love me ? does the unborn girl child many a times ask

Given any responsibilities, she can beautifully complete all her task.


Love is what holds our heart so safe and help us  in life to sail

Love is a blessing of the Creator , without which we all would fail


A priceless question is asked by all who crave for peoples love

To love all men is to love the Lord,  this will kindle happiness in all cove .

# 59

# RUSTIC RADHA OR STYLISH SITA

Girls are such a blessing on Mother Earth
Be it family or friends , of happiness there will be no dearth

Villagers may not always rejoice in the news of her birth
To be a female is nothing less virtuous for the human exile on earth

Our Radha may be rustic, with her beauty so rural
And Sita may be stylish , in this world so cruel!

Academic, sincerity, sports and space
She excels everywhere with profound success in every place

To respect women must be taught at every home
Gentlemen or lady we all should realize and practice this on our own,

Why are night duties not very suitable for the female gender
Whoever said that must have experienced substandard behavior , I wonder !

Why in a country cannot Radha walk safely in the dark?
 She might have needed some extra hours to complete her work

May all Radha ,Sita, Seema and Nazma have a personality so bold
Let the Universe help them reach their goal leaving all obstacles behind them to hold!

# 60

# LITTLE PIECE OF RHYMING LITERATURE

Happy was the king, yet he smiled so little

Busy was the doctor , yet he worried so little

Fast was the runner ,yet he ate so little

Swift was the driver, yet he slept so little

Winner was the dancer, yet she sang so little,

Peaceful was the shopkeeper , yet he talked so little.

Tired was the farmer, yet he rested so little,

Poor was the fisherman, yet he sulked so little

Diligent was the teacher, yet he earned so little,

Cute was the child, yet he waved his hands so little

Colourful was the bird, yet it flew so little,

The bird in the cage used to talk a lot, yet it sang so little !!

# 61

## A GIANT FLAW

Today, we consider it a Himalayan blunder when someone decides to study not science but arts

If it is such, from where would have time tested literature emerged and become our life's part?

Appreciation is all that cheers up any candidate

Music wins hearts all over the world and short stories also do consolidate

Flaw lies where we turn a blind eye to the diversities of the subjects

To create new things and derive happiness from them is taught by dance, music, and drawing of objects

Vast is the variation of curricular streams

Becoming famous or a Nobel laureate is what is every societies well cherished dream

Giant flaw occurs when we are a victim of external pressure

Even Angels cannot help you decide if you do not think in leisure

Music , arts and literature are enormously charming

Which allows to leave their marks in time and is also very heart warming

One may not know how to operate or manage a case of seizure

But his artistic works can bring in a fortune and also the painter gain some pleasure.

# 62

## MYOPIC VISION

Spare the rod and spoil the child
Is a line from time unknown
Ignoring his mistakes may turn him wild
Little did his parents realize how fast will time be gone

Today's small errors can take gigantic shape
If you have a myopic vision towards your child's future
He will soon become ill mannered not knowing how to behave
So parents should take control of improving their child's nature

Today if we teach him to plant a tree,
Tomorrow he may not go and cut one
Today if you teach him how to be happy
Tomorrow he will know how to smile even if some of his work is not done

If you teach him that man make money
He will learn not to run after only economy
If we teach him that we eat to live
He will learn the art to share and give

Please use some spectacles for the eyes of your souls
Cure your myopic vision and let us all achieve our goals!!

# 63

## PASSIVE VOICE

The survival of the fittest is the truth that we have known
So what happens to the unfit, the broken, the unwanted, should they all be thrown?

Who worthily deserves it is so doubtful, patiently awaits the crown
The winner  may be wearing a dhoti or she may be wearing a gown

The poor have nothing to say, all sing the same age old lullaby
The villages still get drowned in floods or intimidated by any bossy city man saying "Hi"

Their nights are still dark and lands still dry
Literacy is their dream,who is there to hear their cry?

As civilization proceeds, so increases deforestation
Very few trees are later planted with little hope of greeneries restoration

Time and tide will wait for none
Speak up for what is right or the precious today will quickly be gone

Non cooperation is active a deed
Although passive sounds its initiation indeed

Plant some trees and save some water
Spread some education , electricity and good culture

Let the poor survive, the oppressed breath in some fresh air
Mentally disturbed people and loners also get some love and care

Not all can identify or stand against what is wrong

A passive and weak voice if put together with others can become very promisingly strong

# 64

## THAT THIRSTY CROW

Once upon a time there was a crow so thirsty

His wisdom lead to some new ideas that helped him to get some water

It  helped the crow and also taught us a lesson

That a work done on time gives results much better

But if the drops of water cannot quench your thirst

What else would you do to become the very first

Greed is something that has always tried to destroy us

But the greedy men will never realize this lesson from his class

The more you get, the more you want

True is the saying, some men do not change, some men cannot change even if they want

Earning , prizes or cars be it

Properties are blissful unless they make us develop more greed

Time teaches everything , like living and loving

Greed once developed, you cannot get rid of it, for that you hae to be very daring

Need or greed , we ourselves have to decide

With a very perfect preference, shall peace always precide

Lives are lost, lotteries are devastating

Greed should be avoided even if it is so luring

Thirst like greed if not quenched , shall give us trouble so immense

The cause of polydipsia can be treated, but greed is incurable until cured by our senses!

# 65

## A THING LIKE LOVE

To fall in love was not by choice
He was fascinated by her style and her voice

Yet they never talked to each other
Both of them never knew each others thoughts and had nothing to chatter

She fell in love with his bright eyes
Yet she did not know how it would suffice

Unveiled feelings and unhampered emotions
Seasons change and so changes every man's resolution

Some got married and osme got diverged away in separate path
To strike a discordant note was not what they nurtured in their heart

His heart skipped a beat to see her leisurely walk
No one ever saw them to sit and talk

To love is like to see a beautiful tree grow
Watering always and allowing all fruits and flowers to show

To give is to love, and to go beyond limits
Those who do not know what is love is nothing but timids

It is not explained by any relation or possession
It is decided by realization, support and devotion

To get and to forget is not our motto
To love, give and forgive shall keep us running in toto.

# 66

## AS THE SKY IS BLUE

We stand under a blue sky so vast

With good memories and hopes for long to last

The sky is blue with floating clouds

Over the moon we feel to gain freedom from every defying shroud

Where the thought of every kind can silently wander

We love the floating clouds, even though they sometimes bring thunder

Freshness of a wide smile indeed comes for free

First breath when one took, it seemed to be the much awaited key

Courageous heart and audacious nature

In an absolute way they can augment your stature

As light as a feather your heart will feel

By your resolute stands, your personality will not be as intricate as appears your deal

A rusty mind like gusty wind

Shall break all barriers and create a story of mysterious kind

Fears like termites can destroy our dreams architecture

A gallant character shall act like a savior of the vigorous endeavor

# 67

# GREENSTICK OR A DISPLACED FRACTURE

With an impact so meager to begin with

It appeared to us like a non tormenting greenstick fracture

In a northern neighboring country it showed its initial sparks

With time it spread like wild fire and left everything behind dark


A massive injury to human resource it was beyond any doubt

One after another it affected peoples life, hovering over the country's economy like a dark cloud

It shattered peoples hopes , plans and travels for many days

Like a comminuted fracture , it tremendously hurt people globally in every way


It became life threatening and handshake was defied by every dignitary

Greeting from a distant became a norm, wearing a mask became mandatory

Sanitizers and hand washing became compulsory

Health hazards could be controlled by measures practiced unostentatiously


Like emergency casts and slabs were swiftly prepared many urgent hospital beds

Isolation wards and ever developing treatment protocols cured majority, although some were found dead

Country's population faced a grave disaster as bad as a displaced fracture

But doctors, police and all public servants behaved like plates, screws and plaster.


After few desired episodes of lockdown,

The multiplication of pandemic cases started to slow down
The post peak graph line is now declining slowly
Now some people can go out and enjoy sunshine lovingly

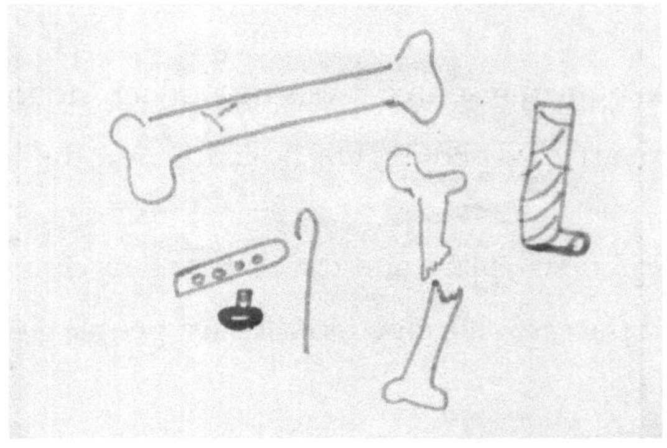

# 68

## WHEN BIRDS USED TO SING IN SPRING

In a note so high, the birds used to sing by

Dawn was heralded by its beautiful tone

Spring was the season of a musical symphony by birds of many  variety

Today we see some scarcity , we have committed  some mistakes that cannot be undone,


Mobile network tower frequencies and waves may alter their flights

Damaging the greeneries are only worsening our plight

Instead of crops, birds today may pick up some pin, glass or plastic

Pollution is generating a red signal , dangerous times it may bring so drastic


Fresh air and slow winds would refresh our tasteless minds

Smog, smoke and fog separately are disasters of a different kind

Even these lead to difficult journey by plane

A single mistake to touch a  flying bird , will make all efforts go in vain


To save the nature is a duty of virtue

We don't neither need to spend any money nor  build a statue

All we need is to determine to dispose, reuse and recycle

Plant some trees, save the fuel,and try to ride some bicycle


The plants and trees give us oxygen from all time

If we damage them , we are sure to bring us an ominous time

Oxygen cylinders and  oxygen bars will become a necessity

Before we reach the point of no return, let us make planting trees an urgent priotrity

# 69

# WHEN OSTRICHES RUN

The fastest running bird is ostrich, a well known fact it is,

Largest bird egg does it produce, an interesting point it is

The opulent like  the ostrich can run very fast in the society

Like the successful stars, important position holders, and the rich get all the priority

The people in silk stockings wear deep pocketed jackets

About the insolvent they are least concerned , even if  they are creating some unknown rackets

Nepotism and colleges run by high capitation fees are not the actual problem

Unless you rip apart some other person's wonderfully vivid dream

Humans are we and not mere topper like ostriches

To value others desires and make space for others giving them equal privileges

Competition begets dedication, no doubt about that

But satisfaction is a reward more renowned did we ever ponder about that?

Racism , troubles and domineering people always make companionship so undermined,

Such difficulties should be avoided and  overcome with time, for this we shall be determined.

# 70

## THE FEARS OF A PESSIMIST

A diamond is found in a mine of coal,

Does the world have any space for a misanthrope?

An optimist tries to see the non existing light

A pessimist tries to blow off the gleaming light

I and you should be atleast an optimist if not out and out a philanthrope!


The story of the glass of water half full or half empty

Is a question evoking argument in many,

Which one is the correct answer is yet to be decided

Both the answers are correct and the judgment doesn't differ by a single penny!

But the outlook is what we have to select

If to think like an archivist or focus only on the defect


Struggle is always present in one stage of our life or the other

Everyone has faced the scuffle, be it you yourself or your father

To look beyond the tussle is every optimist's quality

 A pessimist is sure to be disappointed, not able to perform any duty

An optimist makes use of every situation for his own good

Leaving no stone unturned is a conduct developed that will help us in every mood!

# 71

## BAREFOOT

Water is life,so do many say,

Drop after drop is somewhere wasted, some water by chance flows away

All places do not have water supply so regular

Miles after miles they have to walk on foot to collect water, so eager

Surplus be the water supply in all places of the country

Paucity and poverty makes them feel the real water scarcity

When hunger is belt tightening for days at a stretch

Working and walking barefoot is no longer a big challenge

The affluent and the prosperous can try not to waste a drop

Little  better water supply can help the farmers grow some better crop

The plight of the villagers in some areas are miserable

They know the worth of every drop of water that is collectable

Pauperism and indigence cannot be improved so early

Take small steps , one by one can bring in some changes very clearly.!

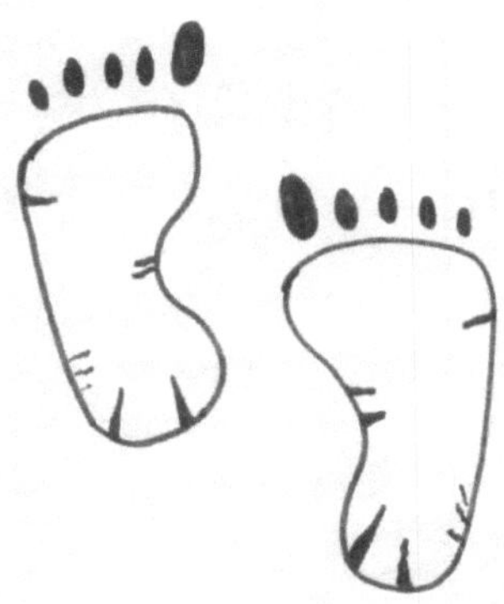

# 72

## POTTER POTION

His scar left a mark on our childhood memories

Potter series could indeed take away all our agony

Lily's love as a mother, the role of the character Snape

Was so beautifully narrated , we experienced a world outside which we never wanted to escape

Having friends like Ron and Hermione, Harry must have felt lucky

The villain created all devastations, everyone felt helpless and feary

Hagrid was a warm hearted person, and a great Headmaster like Dumbledore

A teacher like professor McGonagal,what one can ask for more

The constant small conflicts and never ending fight,

Always Harry remembered his mother and how Hagrid hugged him very tight

Sirius Black and the Weasley's family have been of a support so immense

Harry Potter apart from his scar and parseltongue had a life full of blessing

Like Harry, can every other person can fight against all evil

Love of family and friends can strengthen everyone's will

An orphan was the chosen hero, he became the protagonist

The devil brute 'you know who'', Lord Voldemort had many names on his list

Victory of good over evil is what happened in the end

All was possible by a young boy , his constant supporters and his wand

The invisibility cloak, the Marauder's map, and exciting was weasley's extendable ears

Hedwig ,Crookshanks and patronus of varied patterns was indeed so dear

Spells, curses, the sorting hat and the forbidden forests

Flying cars, platform 9 3/4 ,magical was the journey for many it is the dearest!

9¾
COMMON
ROOM

# 73

# THE TALKING CLOCK

A miracle of researchers it was indeed
Creating a clock that would talk
It was a boon for many
Mainly for those who carried a blind stick to walk

When worn on the wrist it is appears to be a wrist watch
Watch when thought about points us to be careful
The importance of time is indicated by watches of all kind
We should utilize time properly as life can be very dutiful

A talking clock was once a luxury
Today within mobiles and digital clocks it has become a necessity
Benefits of this scientific creation
Was a wonder made out of constant devotion

The first of its kind was used to be imported
Now in many countries they are manufactured
The talking clock make people wonder
How powerful is time to which everyone has to surrender!

# 74

## THE MEN IN MASKS

Dress code changed when the pandemic started

Along with buying sanitisers frequently,variety of masks are carted

Some wore triple layered masks so unique

Some used cloth mask so definite

All health care workers were used to wearing

N -95 masks while they were working

It was a life and death question,

Taking precautions were the only solution

Make up kits and lipsticks lost their use

Many people developed depression and loneliness with nothing to amuse

One fine morning shall it also be over

We pray all can restart their normal lifestyle to last forever

The medical staff , the sweeper, policeman and all those who fought like brave warriors

Their names will be remembered with great respect as they are the history makers!

# 75

# IDENTITY CRISIS

Why not we love ourselves , and give up all the envy?

Self respect and respect for others will no doubt make a good story

Narrating success stories and pompous prosperity

Cannot create a long lasting image, if you do not practice charity

Looking down upon the underpriviledged section

Feeling jealous of others upliftment will increase all the tension

Thoughts if full of dishonor and distaste

If there persists identity crisis , our lives will be just a waste

Psychology says to accept yourself and cause no further damage

Live and let live well does the saying go,

Grow and let grow shall be the notion to follow

To help others cannot be made compulsory

But not to harm others should be included in the advisory.

# 76

## INTERNSHIP DAYS

Long awaited days are finally here

Last semester exams result were declared and most of them have cleared

In a profession like medical, where judgment is so critical

Internship days like a spell, made everyone feel so well,

New roosters were made ,new stethoscopes selected,

Junior doctors association was formed and their leader was elected

New patients to examine, new cases to study

New friends to be made how charming is all that buddy?

Emergencies were neatly attended, casualties taken care of

Minor procedures were learnt, to meet patients' demands we are always there for

Further exams were pending  , we had many further plans so tempting

Curriculum was curious, internship days were all so serious

It all ended very soon,memories created appeared like a boon

The last day there was a program arranged of very good a taste

All took part and, a wonderful night was witnessed without any haste

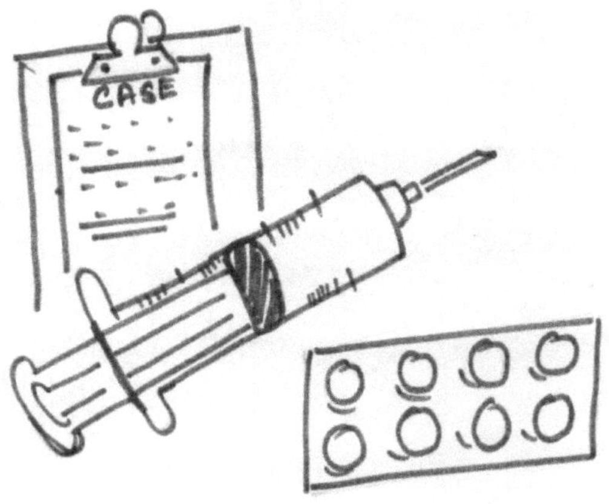

# 77

# A REPORTER'S RECORD

Many risk —taking, life-staking responsibilities they shoulder

Reporters are they whose pens record things from petty pebbles to big boulders

The news from the NASA and media coverage of a mission to moon

Biggest tsunami is recorded and weather forecasting correctly is done very soon

They reach the country's border and record the army's valor

Collecting information of  breaking bridges, lives lost and army's glamour

From years their role has been considered so important

And for years to come will their recorded things e securely present

Terrorists termination and failing projects are all brought to light

A reporter's voice and their pens always leave a mark so right

Largest architecture ,awesome means of transport

The journalists capture them all and make a big report

Fourth pillar of democracy indeed do they  form

With their contribution can we be protected from impending storm

Ominous mishaps, doctors dejection, researchers requests are all well focused

The reports do face all the stuff and pick up the topic to be well discussed

A reporter's records gather news from every sphere as much as they can

The common man loves their response and many of  them have become their fan

# 78

## HEADACHE

Physically when you are tired or suffer from headache

Medicines can cure them and then you can enjoy a milkshake

But what is the solution to a headache so virtual

When behavior and values are camouflaged to a bigger scale

Insincerity in the smallest way and lies always makes a way

Truth is sometimes subdued, foul games make our decisions sway

To make a fool of someone is a motto of many men

All use a bait to kill a lion by bringing him out of his den

Head carries the brain  within , thoughts arise of virtue and sin

Disgrace goes to the people who select mistaken ways leading to ruin

Clear be our thoughts, bonafide be our actions

Headache will get resolved without any malicious detection

# 79

# WHAT WINNING WOMEN WONDER

When she strives to make great strides

 A winner she will become one day, depending on what she decides

Colossal company of family and friends, their enormous efforts

Helped her bloom into a magnificent personality as say all their reports

Checked and cross checked were all her answers

Wonderfully and correctly were they written, that would startle all examiners

Swimming against the tide she made her progress

A day she dreams of achieving her desired success

A woman she was she realized very soon,

A tough fight it was indeed and many duties to be done

Criticism and blame game would pull her back

From sports , lonely travel and yearning for prizes to adorn her rack

Success stories of many women would boost her self confidence

Proceeding step by step would give her joy so immense

Why all women can't become a supernova

Wonders many people,is the hope for the remaining women over?

Whether ,men or women should not ignite a debate

May her qualities be recognized and respected at an optimum rate

Like widow remarriage and Sati abolishment

Let their emerge strict rules of women education

So all aspects of villagers will also be benefited

Well men can always succeed and women will not feel adjudicated !

# 80

## GOODBYES ARE DIFFICULT

Introduction, like a new beginning is so charming
New hopes,new preparation and its all about new bonding

Friends or relations you get to know each other
Time and tide nothing at all seems to bother

Heart is charged , soul feels encouraged
Duties done and relaxation goes well played

Splendid will be the time spent so preciously
But at times we need to let go of stuff indecisively

All of a sudden , may be for a reason
Good byes appear from nowhere, unaware of any season

Tears roll down and emotions turn sour
We do not know if the incoming thoughts are ours

Aching hearts , throbbing head, pounding pulses
Today you are reminded of the day you first exchanged glances

A time of bidding farewell, a time to say goodbye
Difficult it is indeed, for the fearless, angry, coward or the shy!

It is a book of


Some poems, very simple

Rhyming randomly,

Presented prayerfully,

Prepared with perspiration,

Desired with dedication

Expecting some acceptance


Thank you for your tolerance!


For my readers: - thank you for your interest and blessings